# Love Puppies

WE'RE HERE
TO HELP!

## Dream Team

### By JaNay Brown-Wood

SCHOLASTIC INC.

*To all the coaches who taught me what teamwork really means. And to the Rainbow Rangers—one pup-tastic soccer team!*

Copyright © 2023 by JaNay Brown-Wood

Interior illustrations by Eric Proctor, © 2023 Scholastic Inc.

All rights reserved. Published by Scholastic Inc., *Publishers since 1920.* SCHOLASTIC and associated logos are trademarks and/or registered trademarks of Scholastic Inc.

The publisher does not have any control over and does not assume any responsibility for author or third-party websites or their content.

No part of this publication may be reproduced, stored in a retrieval system, or transmitted in any form or by any means, electronic, mechanical, photocopying, recording, or otherwise, without written permission of the publisher. For information regarding permission, write to Scholastic Inc., Attention: Permissions Department, 557 Broadway, New York, NY 10012.

This book is a work of fiction. Names, characters, places, and incidents are either the product of the author's imagination or are used fictitiously, and any resemblance to actual persons, living or dead, business establishments, events, or locales is entirely coincidental.

ISBN 978-1-338-83410-9

10 9 8 7 6 5 4 3 2        23 24 25 26 27

Printed in the U.S.A.        40

First printing 2023

Book design by Omou Barry

Decorative design border art © Shutterstock.com

# TABLE OF CONTENTS

# Fall in love with each paw-fectly sweet adventure!

# Chapter 1
# Puppy Play

"Hup, hup! Go loooooong!" shouted Barkley just before he took flight.

Barkley was no regular dachshund puppy—he was one of the magical Love Puppies. And his special skill was transformation, which he had used to turn himself into a purple Frisbee. His friend Rosie, a golden retriever, was currently holding him gently between her teeth. With a flick of her head, Rosie let go of Frisbee-Barkley and he flew through the air.

"Send him my way, Noodles!" called Clyde the Shar-Pei. Noodles, a labradoodle, used her magic to whip up a wind. Frisbee-Barkley twirled and floated right up to Clyde, who used his power of flight to soar up into the sky and catch the purple Frisbee with his paws. With a flying flip, Clyde landed on the ground, Frisbee-Barkley in tow.

"Now that was un-Fris-bee-lievable!" called Clyde with a yip.

Rosie grinned and activated her own flower magic, sending a shower of petals dancing over her Love Puppy team. Each of the puppies giggled and nipped at the twirling petals. Then they fell into a doggie pile, overcome with joyful laughter.

"What should we do now, Pups?" asked Rosie. The pups rested under the warm sun in the backyard of their Love Puppy Headquarters. Rosie lay on the top of the pile, belly up.

"We could play a game of 'What's That Smell?'" said Clyde.

"Nah," said Barkley as he transformed back into his regular body. "With Noodles's new nose, she could smell almost anything from ten miles away."

It was true. After one particular Love Puppy mission, Noodles's nose had changed into the shape of a heart and glowed whenever she felt strong emotions. It also heightened her ability to smell and helped her know if someone was in need.

And Rosie, who was the leader of the puppies, had gained a new talent, too. A heart on her chest glowed vibrantly to alert her to children who needed the Love Puppies' special brand of help. It also let her keep an eye on friends they helped in the past. All she had to do was activate the glowing heart and it allowed for her to check in on those friends, just like a window into their lives. So far, all the humans they had assisted in previous missions were doing very well.

As for Clyde and Barkley, they hadn't developed any new powers. Yes, Clyde could fly and Barkley could transform into just about anything. Not to mention that when they combined their powers with Noodles's and Rosie's, they could open the Doggie Door portal, giving them entrance to the human world.

But other than that—no new superpowers for those two.

"How about we eat a nice tuna fish sandwich?" asked Clyde.

"We just *ate* lunch, silly pup," responded Rosie.

"Did we?" said Clyde. The giant bowl of Bones and Bits he had just finished up had clearly slipped his mind.

"Well, maybe we could—" began Barkley, but he stopped mid-sentence. Right at that moment, Noodles's nose glowed bright orange and Rosie's chest heart illuminated pink.

"Guess we won't be needing something to do," said Rosie, jumping to her feet. "Looks like we've got a new mission. Come on, Pups! Let's head inside."

They knew that the Crystal Bone would be flashing and vibrating with urgent news of the next mission. All the puppies jumped right up and chased after Rosie.

Except for Barkley. He hadn't moved. He stayed back for a moment more, scratching at his ear with his hind leg.

Usually, new missions got Barkley so excited. But even with the possibilities of this new adventure, Barkley could not help but wonder if he'd ever get a new gift like Rosie and Noodles had.

Would he learn something new about himself that would open up a new talent for him to share with the Love Puppy team? Without a new talent, would he really be helpful to the already powerful team of pooches?

"Come on, Barkley Boy," called Rosie, who had already made it to the front door.

With that, Barkley bounded her way, pushing the thought out of his mind.

# Chapter 2
# Mission Eliana

When Barkley burst through the door, light bounced off the walls of the Doghouse. Between Noodles's nose, Rosie's heart, and the blinking of the Crystal Bone, Barkley wondered if this is what it felt like to be at one of the discos he had read about in stories.

The pups followed the Crystal Bone as it floated from the front door, through the hallway, and into the living room.

Being magical puppies came with many perks. Like living in an enchanted Doghouse that took care of all their needs. Whenever the pups were hungry, they had a choice of whipping something up themselves, which they often did since Clyde and Rosie loved to cook. *Or* the pups could just step into the kitchen and speak what they wanted.

"Ham sandwich, please"—*poof* and it materialized right in front of their feet.

"Doggie bone and bacon soufflé if you wouldn't mind"—*poof.*

Even the headquarter's decor was enchanted—like the animated banners that hung from the ceiling. They had pictures of each puppy that barked and played and interacted with the real puppies.

Noodles blew a gentle breeze to greet the banner-pups as the Love Puppies entered the living room, and the banner-pups danced across their fabric with delight.

All the other rooms were enchanted, too. Bathroom showers that turned on as soon as they stepped on the mat. Water that mixed with shampoo, conditioner—whatever they needed—and rinsed over their fur. Back scrubbers that rubbed just right and cleaned them from nose tip to tail.

Bedrooms with doggie-beds that made themselves.

A playroom that switched out the toys, based on what the pups were feeling.

A library that played audiobooks or music whenever the Love Puppies liked.

But one of the best things the pups could ask for was the Crystal Bone. It was a magical crystalline bone that alerted the team of their new missions. It glowed and flashed, levitated and buzzed. And when the pups were ready to learn about their next adventure, Rosie would place her paws on the Bone to get the details.

Which was exactly what she was doing at that very moment.

"Let's see who needs us today," called Rosie. She stood on her hind legs with both paws placed softly onto the slick surface of the Bone. She closed her eyes and listened. Sometimes the Bone projected a video onto the ceiling or created a hologram for the pups to watch. Other times it sent information right into Rosie's mind.

This time, it projected images onto the ceiling like a giant movie playing out, scene by scene.

Each pup stared up at the ceiling, waiting to learn who they would be helping today. The Bone projected some information:

**NAME: ELIANA CONTRERAS SILVA**
Age: Eight
Grade: Third
Problem: Trying out for the basketball team for the first time

The pups watched Eliana in action. In one video, Eliana dribbled the ball up and down the asphalt, bouncing it through her legs as she ran.

"Whoa!" said Barkley.

The next video showed Eliana shooting baskets and barely missing any, making shot after shot, one after the next. Another video showed Eliana dribbling the ball while being guarded by a different person. Eliana moved one way, then the next, dribbling the ball like it was a part of her body. Then she sped past the person guarding her and laid the ball into the basket.

"She's pup-tastic!" called Clyde.

"Yeah," agreed Noodles. "I don't really see why she needs our help."

"Hmmmm," said Rosie, her paws still on the Bone. "There's more."

The pups watched now as Eliana dribbled the ball down the court. There were others on her team that were wide open, but Eliana shot the ball anyway—*swish*. This happened over and over and over again.

"Interesting," said Barkley. His tail got to wagging as he watched, which was kind of strange since he still didn't feel excited about this mission. But the sensation in his tail quickly changed to an itch, which he scratched with his paw until the itchiness went away.

At this point, it wasn't clear how this young girl needed the pups' help.

The next images showed Eliana snatching the ball from others. "Try to keep up!" she called.

Even though she made basket after basket, the pups never saw her pass the ball even one time to her teammates. She also never had anything nice to say, except about herself.

"She's really, really good," said Barkley.

"Yeah," said Noodles. "She's so talented!"

"We've never had a mission like this before," said Rosie. "Usually, it's pretty easy to know what is needed." She sat on the ground with all four paws down.

Barkley's itch returned, but this time it was on his ear. He scratched gently as he sat. "Do you think she'll make it onto the team?" he asked.

"I don't know," answered Rosie, coming over and extending her paw to scratch behind Barkley's ear. "Better?" she asked as Barkley sighed with relief.

"Yes, much better," he responded. Thankfully, the itch went away.

"Well," Rosie continued, "the Bone said that tryouts begin today—right now!"

"Then, it sounds like that's our first step in this mission," said Barkley. "Go check her out in person and figure out what we can do to help."

"In that case . . ." began Rosie. She and all the pups stood in a circle and placed their paws in the middle, their paw pads glowing brightly.

"With the power of love—anything is possible. Love Puppies, go!"

*Whoosh!*

# Chapter 3
## She's Got Skills

The Love Puppies landed with a soft *thud* behind a group of bushes not too far from an elementary school blacktop. They were in perfect earshot to hear what was happening on the court but still out of sight of any humans.

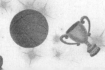

As magical puppies, they always had to work to not be spotted by unsuspecting humans. Being seen made for so many cuddles and too many questions.

The four pups huddled side by side, peering through their bushy hiding place. A group of young girls bounced balls and shot baskets on the blacktop.

"There she is," whispered Barkley. The pups located Eliana. Her brown hair was pulled back into a short ponytail and her kind, light brown eyes focused on the basket. Even though there were many other girls nearby, Eliana kept to herself, shooting the ball and chasing after it to retrieve it.

She didn't seem sad or shy or scared. She actually seemed quite confident on the court. But she also didn't smile or talk at all, like the other girls did as they practiced.

"Has anyone figured out just what she needs help with yet?" whispered Clyde.

Each pup shook their head.

"It looks like tryouts are just getting started," said Rosie. "That should help us get the answers we need."

At that moment, a tall man wearing a baseball cap walked onto the court. He blew a loud whistle, which hung from a cord around his neck. His collared, short-sleeved shirt was tucked into shiny pants that swished as he walked. He was joined by an even taller woman, who also wore a cap and held a clipboard.

"Those must be the coaches," said Noodles. "Why else would they be wearing matching outfits?"

"Maybe they're a crime-fighting duo," said Clyde with a chuckle.

"I doubt it, silly pup," said Rosie, ruffling Clyde's fur and giggling. She turned her attention back to the coaches.

"Let's get started, girls!" the man called, his voice booming. "Go ahead and put your basketballs in that bag and line up on the sideline.

Then sign your name on this clipboard."

The girls followed his directions and lined up next to one another, facing the coaches. Each girl signed the sheet of paper clipped to the board and passed it along.

Eliana followed suit, just like the others.

"Well, she doesn't have a problem taking directions," said Barkley. "That's good if you want to be on a team."

As she stood by the other girls, it was obvious that she was much younger than many of them. And much smaller. Only two other girls were shorter than her—probably other third graders.

The man started up again once the clipboard

was passed to him. "I'm Coach Wong and this is Coach Hampton," he said, gesturing to the woman who stood beside him. "Welcome to Day 1 of tryouts for the Lady Gators basketball team. This week, you're going to get a chance to show us your stuff. Yes, we're looking for girls with skill," he said, "but we're also looking for heart, hustle, and awesome teamwork. You ready to show us what you got?"

All the girls cheered, except Eliana. Her face was serious, and her eyes seemed to be glued to the coach like nobody else was there. She still didn't smile but pulled her arms across her chest, stretching her muscles.

"Today, we've got some returning players trying out to keep their spots on the team— fourth, fifth graders," Coach Wong continued. "But we have some new faces, too, since third graders are allowed to try out this year. Okay, let's do roll call to help me learn names."

The coach began reading out names and checking them off each time a girl raised her hand.

"Next, Eliana Contreras Silva . . ." he said, then stopped. He looked at her as she raised her hand. "Contreras Silva," he said again. Eliana looked down at her shoes and lowered her hand. "Not Contreras Silva like *Marianna* Contreras Silva?"

All the other girls turned to stare at Eliana who still watched her own feet like her life depended on it.

"What's going on?" whispered Noodles. Her nose glowed as they watched Eliana's body tense. Something was definitely up.

Finally, Eliana spoke up: "Yes. That's my sister."

"Well now," said the coach, clapping the clipboard excitedly. "Marianna is off at that university across the country playing like a pro! Even though it's her first year! I've been following her—she's got professional basketball written all over her."

Eliana nodded slowly, her frown dipping deeper on her face.

"Congratulations to her! I sure am excited to see what you've got, Eliana," he said before finally moving to the next girl in line.

"I don't think she liked that at all," said Barkley. Eliana still hadn't looked up from the ground.

"Okay, girls, let's start with some sprints," Coach Wong called once he made it all the way through the line. "Line up on the baseline and when we say go, run across the court to the other baseline and then back. We'll do this a few times to get all warmed up. Ready . . ."

*TWEET!*

At the blow of his whistle, the girls took off at full speed, hurtling down the court to the other side and quickly turning back around to return. Eliana was at the front of the pack. She pumped her arms and clenched her fists, looking down the line to see if anyone was ahead of her.

*TWEET* went the whistle and off went Eliana.

"Good job!" The coaches clapped after a few sprints. "Grab some water."

The girls breathed hard, gulping deeply from their water bottles. A few gathered together, chatting, but Eliana kept to herself during the break and the team stretch.

And during the drills.

Even during team huddles.

With each new task the coaches gave, Eliana shined. She dribbled faster than the other girls, made more baskets, and ran quicker than anyone else on the court.

"She's doing amazing," whispered Rosie. "She's, like, *really* good."

"Yeah," responded Barkley. "But she doesn't seem to be liking any of it. Not even a bit. I wonder why."

"Bring it in, girls," boomed Coach Hampton with a deep voice as Coach Wong stood beside her. "Nice job today. Since we have way more girls than we expected, we'll have to make our first cuts after Day 2. But as long as you keep working as hard as you are, you'll be just fine," she told the team. Then she flashed a thumbs-up to Eliana, and Eliana nodded slightly.

Even though she was amazing on the court, by the end of practice, something was clear as day to the pups: "Eliana didn't make any friends with her new teammates," said Barkley.

"Well, if that's all she needs, we've got that covered," said Rosie. The pups had successfully helped children make friends plenty of times before.

"It does seem like a good place to start," said Noodles.

"But," began Barkley, "do you need to have friends to make it onto a team?"

That was a good question. The pups had no idea.

# Chapter 4
# Passing on Friendship

Back at the Doghouse, the puppies readied their materials.

"Making friends may at least help Eliana to have more fun out there," said Rosie, "and that could boost her chances of making the team—right?"

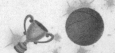

"Makes sense to me," said Clyde.

"I think a letter with a gift is a good idea," said Rosie. "It may not have worked perfectly in the past—"

"You mean it led to a garden disaster!" Noodles reminded everyone while snickering.

"Yes, but that was because the girls didn't know each other. In this case, Eliana has at least met all the girls trying out for the team."

"True," said Barkley. "What should we have her give as a gift?"

"Flowers are good," said Rosie. She looked around the room at the blooms growing in small pots, lining the windowsills. Then she wiggled her nose causing the flowers to dance. "They are *always* a perfect gift."

"Something nice to wear is a good gift, too," said Barkley.

"Or something to eat," added Clyde. "That makes the *best* type of gift."

"What if we tried a little bit of a mix?" asked Rosie. "Though, not the food, of course. Sorry, Clydie. Some of the girls might have allergies."

Clyde shrugged. "Just means more for me."

"What do you have in mind, Rosie-Posie?" asked Noodles.

"I know!" said Barkley. "Remember when we all got enchanted friendship necklaces made out of magic and light?" Each of the puppies gently touched their necks where the necklaces of light hid beneath their fur. After that special mission, their combined magic had created these beautiful necklaces that only they could see. "Well," continued Barkley, "what if we made friendship bracelets out of flowers?"

"Daisies would be perfect for that!" said Rosie, her tail dancing. "Barkley and Noodles, you type the letter. Clydie and I will get to the bracelets."

"How many should we do?" asked Clyde.

"Three seems like a good number. We can see which girls talk with Eliana the most during practice—"

"If any do," interjected Barkley. He wasn't sure if this was the best approach.

"It's worth a try, right, Barkley Boy?" asked Rosie.

He nodded at her words, but a twinge of guilt fluttered inside him. Not only did he not have a great new talent, but sometimes, his ideas seemed to put a damper on the puppies' plans.

The familiar itch came back, but this time it tickled the back of his neck. He shook his head and brought his mind back to his task.

"You ready, Barkley?" asked Noodles, holding three sheets of paper.

Barkley's paws began to glow as his

body morphed into a typewriter.

"Ready," he barked.

In no time, the pups had created three daisy-chain bracelets and three letters. Each one read:

Hi, I'm Eliana.

It's been fun playing basketball
with you. I made you this bracelet.
Do you want to be my friend?

Circle YES or NO

From,

Eliana

"Paw-fect!" called Rosie. "Let's get to tryouts

and put our plan into action!"

\* \* \*

Back outside in the bushes, the pups watched closely as Eliana and the other girls lined up on the sideline. Nobody spoke to Eliana, and Eliana continued to keep to herself.

"Okay, girls," said Coach Hampton after their warm-up sprints. "Today, we're going to practice some passes." The coach explained the drill and demonstrated it with Coach Wong. "Sound good?" she asked the team. "Now I'm going to put you into groups of threes."

Eliana rolled her eyes.

"Did you see that?" whispered Barkley. "She doesn't seem too happy to have to work in teams."

"You sure?" asked Clyde. He had missed Eliana's gesture of dislike.

But the answer to Clyde's question became even clearer when the ball was in Eliana's hand and the coach blew the whistle.

Each time she threw the ball to her teammates, they struggled to catch it. Either Eliana passed it too hard so it sailed into the girls' arms with a *thwap*, or too high so they had to jump and still missed it as it floated over their fingertips. But when they passed the ball to Eliana, things were different.

"She's caught all their passes like it was as easy as pie," said Clyde.

"But is she passing too hard to them on purpose?" asked Barkley. The other pups couldn't tell either.

Once the drill was over, the girls lined up on the sideline again.

"That was a nice effort," said Coach Wong. "Remember, catching a pass is great! But making good passes to a teammate is just as important." Coach looked in Eliana's direction, only she didn't notice since her eyes were back on her own shoes.

"All right, let's play a practice game where you can show us your passing skills." The coaches split the girls into four teams. Two teams played on one half of the court with Coach Wong while the other two played on the opposite side with Coach Hampton.

Eliana was on Coach Hampton's side, and the pups could tell Hampton was watching her closely.

Once again, Eliana shined. She stole the ball. She dribbled. She made point after point after point. Each time her teammates passed her the ball, she scored.

But not even one time did Eliana return a pass. If this practice was to show off passing abilities, Eliana was at the bottom of the puppy-pole.

"Why won't she pass the ball?" asked Clyde. The pups were stumped.

Even though the game didn't shine a nice light on Eliana's passing ability, watching her in action gave the pups a chance to see who passed the ball to *her*. They'd be the perfect candidates to receive Eliana's gift.

While the girls huddled up at the end of practice, the pups put their plan in motion.

Noodles whipped up a fog cloud, which covered Clyde, who flew over and placed the three gifts and letters on three backpacks.

"I double-checked that they were the right bags," he said, "because of the water bottles I saw the girls use."

"Good thinking, Pup," said Rosie.

"Lady Gators—BREAK!" said the collective voices of the girls as Day 2 tryouts ended.

The pups watched as Eliana picked up her stuff and began to walk away. They also watched the three girls—Paisley, Annie, and Deidra—find their gifts and letters and turn their gaze toward Eliana.

"Hey, Eliana," Paisley called, jogging to catch up with her.

Eliana stopped and faced her.

"That's really nice," said Paisley. "My answer is yes."

Eliana stared with confusion on her face. "Your answer about what?"

"This," said Paisley, holding up the letter and her wrist that now had a daisy bracelet wrapped around it. She smiled widely. "I got your letter. Yes, I'll be your friend."

Eliana shook her head. She could see two other girls standing a few feet away, also holding letters with the same kind of bracelets on their wrists.

"I didn't make those. Or write any letters," she said. "I don't even know what you're talking about."

"But it says it's from you." Paisley lifted the letter. The pups could hear the hurt in her voice.

"I don't know who gave you that," said Eliana.

"But I'm not here to make friends. I'm just trying to become a basketball player so I can get out of this dumb place. Just like my sister!" With that, Eliana turned around and walked away.

Paisley and the other girls turned to one another. They pulled the bracelets off, ripped up the letters, and tossed them into the nearest wastebasket. Then they grabbed their stuff and headed in the opposite direction of Eliana.

So much for helping her make friends.

# Chapter 5
# A Glimpse Inside

The pups were dumbfounded.

There had been three girls—Paisley, Annie, and Deidra—eager to be Eliana's friend . . . and she turned them down cold.

The Love Puppies sat in silence behind the

bushes, watching Eliana through the gates as she crossed the street.

"I don't get it," said Barkley, scratching away at his chin. "She had three ready-made friends, and she turned them down."

"I don't think this mission is about friendship," said Noodles. "How is she going to make the team if she can't even pass a ball?"

"I think she *can* pass a ball," said Rosie. "She just chooses not to."

"This Eliana is quite a puzzle," said Barkley once his chin had been sufficiently scratched. "If we're going to help her, we've got to find out more."

"When?" said Clyde. "And how?"

"Right now, and by heading *that* way!" said Barkley, pointing after Eliana. Barkley's body began to change. His midsection thinned out, like a sponge that was being squished. As his middle flattened, it stretched until he was the length of a blanket, with his head, legs, and tail sticking out from the edges. "Magic carpet ready!" he said. "Noodles, give us some cloud cover. Let's follow that girl!"

With that, Rosie, Noodles, and Clyde jumped onto Magic Carpet-Barkley. Noodles kicked up a thick cloud, which hid them, and they zoomed skyward in the direction of Eliana.

When they caught up to her, she was turning left and walking down a long street. She dribbled a basketball as she walked. She didn't even look at the ball as she handled it, just *bounce, bounce, bounce* through her legs, around her back, back and forth in front of her body.

From a safe distance, the pups followed her down a cul-de-sac. At the end of the street, a basketball court was set up. A handful of boys played a game of four-on-four against one another, laughing and talking smack.

"There she is, everybody," shouted one of the boys as Eliana approached. "The Third-Grade Thunder."

49

For the first time, the pups saw Eliana smile. It was a wide, bright smile that lit her whole face up like she was staring into the moon.

"Be quiet, Rico," she said, laughing.

"You playing or what?" he asked.

Eliana dropped her backpack and ball on the grass in front of one of the houses and jogged over. "You sure you can keep up?" she said.

The pups parked themselves high in a tree and took in the scene.

Eliana laughed as she played defense against the neighborhood kids. She joked and threw insults, dribbled, and scored point after point.

And she passed the ball over and over again.

And each time she did, it floated into the hands of her teammates.

After the game, they all high-fived one another and parted ways.

"You make the team yet?" asked Rico as he walked with Eliana toward her bag.

"First cuts are posted tomorrow," she said.

"I'm pretty sure you'll make it. They do know you are the little sister of *the* Marianna Contreras Silva, right? The baller that made it out of this place, went to a university, and is dominating. I was watching her game yesterday—*swish*," he said, pretending to shoot a basketball, his hand outstretched above his head with his wrist slightly bent. "Nothing but net!"

"Yeah, nothing but net and leaving her stupid little sister behind," Eliana said, kicking a rock across the street with all her might. It skidded off the asphalt, clacking and bouncing until it hit the grass.

Noodles's nose began to glow.

"Ellie, you know she had to do that. But she'll be back for you. I *know* it."

"Yeah, whatever," Eliana said under her breath, reaching into her pocket and pulling out a key.

"See you tomorrow," said Rico, "and take it easy."

"Bye, Rico," she said.

Rico ran to his house across the street as Eliana went back to hers and stormed through the door.

"Let's get a closer look," whispered Barkley.

The pups headed into Eliana's backyard, the brightness of Noodles's nose leading the way. They stopped at a window and peered inside.

There, they could see Eliana throw her backpack onto the couch and stomp down the hall into another room. Her face was red, and though they couldn't hear what she was saying, they could tell she was fuming.

"Over here," whispered Rosie. She peered into another window.

Eliana stood in her bedroom. She looked up at a large, orange poster. On the poster was a brown-haired young woman in a navy-blue jersey, mid-dribble like the picture had been snapped while she was in action. Across the top said MARIANNA CONTRERAS SILVA in bold white letters. Her jersey had the number 21, and down at the bottom of the poster was the name of the university.

Beside the poster was a blown-up picture of Marianna and Eliana hugging each other. And on the other side of the poster was a picture of Marianna passing a ball to Eliana.

A tear spilled down Eliana's cheek. She

wiped it away, pulled the poster down, and dropped it onto the floor. Then she grabbed an armful of clothes from her bed and charged back into the hallway. The puppies heard a door slam, but they couldn't see the room Eliana had gone into.

The pups stayed by her window for a while—Noodles's nose shining like a hundred-watt bulb—waiting for her to come out.

When she did, her face was calm again—just as Noodles's nose dimmed. Eliana had changed her clothes and her hair was wrapped up in a towel. She stopped and looked down at the poster she had pulled from the wall before her shower. She picked it up and re-taped it to the wall in its original spot, smoothing out any creases it had. Her hand stayed on the poster for a moment longer while she stared at the woman frozen there.

For the rest of the night, Eliana did her homework, made herself something to eat, and then went to bed all by herself in the quiet house. The pups lingered long enough to see a woman in scrubs arrive at the house and unlock the door. After toeing off her shoes, she made her way to Eliana's room. The woman bent over the sleeping girl to kiss her forehead. She had tired eyes, but she smiled a little before quietly exiting the room.

This mission seemed like more than just making the team.

"Pups," said a somber Rosie, "let's head home. We've got some brainstorming to do."

# Chapter 6
# Close Call

Back at the Doghouse, Rosie paced the living

room floor. Barkley sat on his hind legs tracking

her, moving his head as she marched.

He wasn't sure if his idea of following Eliana

had been a helpful one. Instead of giving the

pups the answers they needed to help Eliana make the team, visiting her home had just put everyone in an even more worried mood. *If I had a new talent*, he thought, *maybe that would give me what I need to be more helpful for my puppy teammates.*

At this thought, the obnoxious itch came back, this time tickling itself across all four of his paws. He scratched the best he could, returning his gaze to the obviously concerned Rosie.

"So," Rosie finally said, "her sister left to go play basketball in college."

"Seems so," said Barkley.

"And I think her feelings are hurt because of it," added Noodles, who was lying on her back, sending short bursts of wind to cause the banner-pups to dance with excitement.

"But she passes the ball and smiles when she plays at home," said Clyde in between bites of a bone he was working on while sprawled out on the floor.

"That's the interesting part," said Noodles. "She *can* pass, can even have a good time, when she's with the friends she's known forever."

"I bet she really wants to get on that team to prove something," said Barkley. The other pups yipped in agreement.

"Then, doggone it, what is she missing?" asked Clyde. "She's great at shooting, dribbling, and defending. And she can make a pup-tastic pass when she wants to. Is that enough to make the team?"

"We'll find out tomorrow," Rosie reminded them. "The coaches are making the first round of cuts."

"Is it possible we're too late?" asked Barkley. This concern brought back his urge to scratch again, this time, using both hind legs.

"Barkley Boy," said Rosie, "do you need a bath? You've been awfully scratchy lately."

"I took one this morning," he responded, "but

I just keep itching. Maybe another one wouldn't hurt."

"It's time for bed, anyway," said Rosie. "Pups, think about what we might do to help Eliana. And what plan B may be if she doesn't make the team tomorrow." The pups nodded, then wished one another good night and headed to their bedrooms.

But Barkley made his way to the shower. He stepped on the mat and the water began raining down like one of Noodles's rainstorms. "Body scrub, please," said Barkley.

Metal arms of the enchanted shower stretched down, each with gentle brushes attached at the end. They proceeded to scrub Barkley's ears, head, neck, and back, causing him to relax his shoulders and lean into the sensation. Next, they scrubbed his tummy softly.

Even with the relaxing wash, Barkley's worries still stayed. True, Eliana was good. But she was missing something that was just as important as her skill to make shots or steal balls. Yet, none of the pups had ever been on a sports team. How would they know for sure what she was missing?

Barkley shut off the shower, dried his fur, and hurried to bed.

Tomorrow was a big day for the pups, and for

Eliana. He wanted to make sure he was rested enough to help the poor girl the best he could.

Maybe tomorrow, he'd be a better help to his team than he had been today.

\* \* \*

The next day passed slowly.

The pups still were unclear about what they needed to do to help Eliana. When tryout time came back around, the pups positioned themselves in the same hidden spot behind the bushes.

Right before the school bell rang, they watched as Coach Hampton walked to the wall of the school building that was closest to the blacktop. She pulled out long pieces of masking tape and taped two sheets of paper on the far ends of the wall. Then she walked back into a building just as the bell clanged.

Kids poured out of each of the buildings. A crowd of girls rushed toward the blacktop and then to the wall where the papers were posted. The pups watched as some girls celebrated, pumping their fists with excitement. Others slouched their shoulders and dropped their heads.

Eliana didn't appear until after the crowd thinned out. She stood next to the building, around the corner from where the papers were posted.

She took a big breath and shook her hands as if she was trying to shake water off her skin. Then she walked around the corner and peered up at the sheet. One second, five seconds, ten . . . nothing. She didn't react at all. Next, she turned from the wall and disappeared around the corner.

"Did she make it? Did she make the cut?" asked Clyde. It was like the pups were at the edge of their seats while watching a show full of suspense.

"I can't tell," added Rosie as some more girls left after looking at the papers, either smiling or frowning. "But we definitely can't go over and check yet because more of the girls are coming to see. We'll be spotted for sure."

Barkley's tail wagged wildly. His heart beat in his chest. And just as the group of girls walked away, Barkley burst from the bushes, racing in the direction of the sheet. "I've got to know!" he yelled, charging forward.

"Barkley, wait!" barked Rosie. "You'll be spotted!" As she called after him, another group of girls emerged from a nearby building. Barkley's purple body hurtled toward the wall.

"Oh no!" called Clyde. "I can't watch," he said, dropping to the grass and covering his face with his paws.

In the blink of an eye, Barkley transformed from Puppy-Barkley to Bird-Barkley. He fluttered and reached the roster at the same time as the girls, who pointed and marveled at the pretty purple bird that was close enough for them to touch. Fortunately, they hadn't seen his transformation.

Barkley hovered near the top of the sheet looking at name after name after name. First five names . . . no Eliana. Second five names . . . no Eliana. Nowhere in the top fifteen names did it say "Eliana Contreras Silva."

"Oh no!" tweeted Barkley. "She didn't make it! She didn't make it through the first round of cuts."

# Chapter 7
# Sportsman-what?

Just as Barkley was about to fly back to his team and deliver the news, he saw one last name under the heading ALTERNATE.

The final name on the list stood out loud and clear: Eliana Contreras Silva, the only third grader to make it through the first round of cuts.

But she'd just barely made it. An alternate was not a guaranteed spot.

Barkley zoomed back to the bushes.

"All the way at the bottom," he proclaimed. "That's where her name was."

"Poodle-sticks! The very bottom?" said Rosie.

"Yep. The very last name, under ALTERNATE," Barkley responded.

Even though Eliana had made it to the next round of tryouts, how close she had gotten to being cut felt too close for comfort. The pups had almost failed a mission before they even had a chance to figure out how to help.

And the weight of Eliana's "almost cut" seemed to weigh heavily on her, too. Once Day 3 of tryouts began, Eliana seemed to run slower, try less, and sulk through the drills.

"If she keeps that up, she'll be out for sure!" whispered Barkley.

Her sore attitude lasted for the whole practice, which didn't give the pups much hope.

Once practice was over, the smaller group of girls grabbed their things and began going their separate ways. Eliana did, too, until she was stopped by the loud call of Coach Wong.

"Silva!" he boomed. Eliana froze mid-step. "A word, please."

She turned around and walked back in his direction but kept her head drooped low.

"Chin up, girl," he said. She lifted her eyes and peered into his. "You do know that you almost got cut, right?"

She nodded solemnly.

"You've got skills, Silva. There's no doubt about that. But where's your teamwork? Where's your sportsmanship?"

He paused as if waiting for her to reply. She dropped her gaze again, instead.

"Marianna had wonderful sportsmanship. She was such a great team player—what's your excuse?"

Still, no response.

"Look, if you want to make the team, Hampton and I are going to need to see a real improvement. If you don't adjust your attitude, well, you may have to try again next year." With that, he turned on his heel and walked away.

The puppies could see tears coming down from Eliana's eyes. They knew she'd be heading home to an empty house and a room filled with mementos of her sister. She tightened her backpack and ran from the school grounds, wiping her eyes with her sleeves.

"The Doghouse—now!" said Rosie.

*Whoosh!*

* * *

"Teamwork," said Rosie. "Sportsmanship. That's
it. That's where *we* come in!"

Barkley nodded his head excitedly while the
other pups howled. Finally, they'd figured out
what could possibly turn this all around for
Eliana.

"Teamwork's easy," said Clyde. "That's just
being a good teammate. Like when Rosie helps
to scratch Barkley's ears."

"Or when we all work together to help kids like
Eliana. We're pros at teamwork," said Noodles.
"We Love Puppies are a Dream Team!" she
exclaimed. This sent the puppies into happy

jumps and yips as they tumbled and tickled one another.

"Dream Team for sure!" added Rosie. They gathered in a puppy huddle.

"But what's sportsmanship?" asked Clyde.

Nobody had an answer for that. Rosie hadn't even heard of the word before Mission Eliana. Luckily, she knew who—or what—would know.

"Bone, we need you," she said as she and all the puppies sat back up. "What's sportsmanship?" she asked just before placing her paws onto the Crystal Bone, the magical source for information on all their missions. "Oh, I see," she said. "Show that to the pups, please."

The Crystal Bone projected images of people playing sports together. They smiled and high-fived. They said nice things. They worked together to score points and win.

"*That's* sportsmanship?" asked Clyde. "That just looks like being nice to your teammates."

"I think that's the trick," said Rosie. "It's about respect. Saying nice things."

"Oh, like, 'Rosie, you are looking particularly lovely today,'" said Clyde.

"Aww, thanks, Pup," she replied with a smile.

"I think it's about working together," added Noodles. "Being nice even if you aren't on the same team. Rooting for each other. Like . . . Barkley, you did an amazing job helping us find out if Eliana made the team."

"Thanks," he responded. That did make him feel good. Especially since he still didn't feel so good about not having a new special power. "I bet sportsmanship also means passing the ball just right to your teammate so they can actually catch it," Barkley added. "Or giving other teammates a chance to score, even if you have a really good shot."

Now it was becoming much more apparent why Coach Wong had said what he had. He was right—Eliana had a lot of skills, but no sportsmanship. And her attitude was going to keep her from making the team.

A flood of relief filled the puppies. Finally, they'd figured out what she needed.

Now came the even harder part: figuring out how to help her before it was too late.

# Chapter 8
# To Cheer or Not to Cheer

"So how are we going to help Eliana with sportsmanship?" asked Barkley over dinner. All the brainstorming had made the pups very hungry.

"Well, part of it is cheering for your team,

right? Showing them you are proud of them and excited for what they are doing," said Noodles.

"Yeah," said Clyde, "even if they make a mistake."

"Good thoughts, Pups!" said Rosie. "Let's get Eliana to cheer for her team. That way, she can show her coach that she knows how to be a good teammate—and she's not afraid to show it!"

* * *

The next day of tryouts started like any other. Eliana stole the ball, made some hard shots, and defended well—but never cheered or encouraged her teammates. At water break, Coach Hampton approached the girls with an idea.

"We're going to try something. A cheer-off! I want to see which of you girls has the best team spirit during our next scrimmage. Think you're up to it?"

All the girls cheered, some high-fiving one another. But not Eliana.

The coach split them into teams for a full-court practice game. Eliana wasn't picked as a starter. Instead, she sat on the bench with her lower lip pushed out in a pout.

"Now's our chance to help her show her spirit," whispered Rosie. "How are we going to do it?"

"I've got just the trick," said Barkley. His paws began to glow and his body began to morph.

Soon, he was cone-shaped with a small hole on the top and a large hole at the bottom.

"What a great idea! A Megaphone-Barkley. You are one smart puppy!" said Rosie. "Noodles, can you please make some wind to drop him right beside Eliana on the asphalt?"

"On it," said Noodles. "Just be careful, Barkley!"

Off he went, discreetly floating toward Eliana and landing right next to her hand. The plastic-sounding bump startled her, and she turned her head in the direction of the megaphone.

"Where'd that come from?" she wondered aloud.

"Is that yours?" asked Paisley as she sat beside Eliana on the sideline.

Eliana shook her head. "Never saw it in my life."

"So, you won't care if I use it?" Paisley asked.

"All yours."

Paisley lifted the megaphone to her mouth and began cheering for her team. Her voice echoed across the blacktop causing Coach Wong to look her way. He flashed her a thumbs-up.

"Aww, poodle-sticks!" said Rosie. "That was supposed to help Eliana."

But Eliana continued to sit on the sideline just watching the game, not cheering or clapping at all.

"Go team!" boomed Paisley through Megaphone-Barkley. Eliana leaned away and covered her ears.

"Why don't you ever cheer for your teammates?" asked Paisley, obviously bugged by Eliana's rudeness.

"None of us have made the team yet," said Eliana. "Right now, everybody is my competition."

"But if you make the team, they *will* be your teammates. I know. I was on the team last year. We remember the teammates who work with us—and the ones who don't."

Just then, Coach Hampton pointed to the bench and said, "Paisley, you're in! And excellent cheering, by the way!" she said, slapping her a high five.

As she jumped up to join the game, Paisley dropped the megaphone beside Eliana. "Better cheer up if you want to make this team," said the girl. Then she jogged onto the court.

"You two, you're in as well," said Coach Wong, pointing to two other girls who had been cheering their heads off. He high-fived both of them as they took their places on the court.

"Are the coaches ever going to put Eliana in?" asked Clyde. The team had been playing for a while, but she was still warming the bench.

Eliana eyed Megaphone-Barkley for a moment, sliding her hand closer to him.

The pups held their breaths.

Then Eliana moved her hand away and turned her attention back to the game.

"Oh poo!" said Clyde, folding his paws across his chest.

Back on the blacktop, Paisley got the ball. She dribbled without any effort, and even though she had a clear shot, she passed the ball to Deidra who set, aimed, and fired. *Swish!* Two points followed by high fives all around.

"Nice shot," shouted Paisley.

Eliana continued to watch Paisley move up and

down the court, dribbling, stealing, and passing.

"That Paisley girl is pretty good, huh?" said Clyde.

"She's good at working as part of a team, too. If only Eliana would get the hint," said Rosie.

"Let's bring Barkley back," said Noodles. "Eliana isn't going to use him."

Noodles positioned herself next to the bush to blow a quick burst of tornado-like wind that would suck Megaphone-Barkley back their way. But just as she started, Coach Hampton headed toward the sidelines.

"Who else hasn't been in?" asked Coach. Eliana and two other girls raised their hands.

"All right, Lesley, Luna, and"—she turned to Eliana—"Eliana. You're all in."

"Here's her chance to show them her team spirit," whispered Clyde, waggling his tail.

As soon as she stepped on to the court, it was more of the same: excellent dribbling, excellent shooting, and excellent defense.

But zero passing and zero teamwork.

# Chapter 9
# A Sticky Situation

"Why won't she play as part of the team?" asked Barkley once he'd finally returned safely behind the bushes. "The coach told her it was important, a teammate told her the same thing—what's with Eliana?"

The pups just couldn't put their puppy paws on it.

"Maybe this is another question for the Bone!" said Rosie. Her ears perked up as whistles began to blow, letting the pups know that practice was over. That also meant that Day 4 of tryouts was over, too—and the coaches were that much closer to making the final cuts. "We'd better figure it out soon. Let's head home. Paws in, Pups!"

With the enchanted words and activated magic, the Doggie Door portal opened and the puppies jumped in.

Soon, they were standing inside the Doghouse

living room, eyeing the Crystal Bone.

Rosie placed her paws on it. "Bone, what else can you tell us about Eliana? Why won't she play as part of a team?"

Rosie lifted her paws and cupped them in front of her. A small pink hologram of a much younger Eliana shined in the center of her paws. The pups watched as Eliana and her sister played together—passing, high-fiving, cheering each other on as they practiced by their house. Next, the hologram changed and the pups watched Marianna coach Eliana and a group of other girls, reminding them to cheer for one another. Then Marianna turned to her and said, "We'll always be a team!" and hugged her tightly.

One final hologram scene played on Rosie's paws. Marianna stood outside the house, loading bags into the family's truck. Eliana watched from the front door. "Come here, Ellie," said Marianna, but Eliana didn't move. "Can I have a hug, before I go?" she asked.

"I thought we were a team! Teammates don't leave!" yelled Eliana before turning and storming back into the house.

Marianna's shoulders fell and she sighed deeply. Then she climbed into the van and closed the door.

The hologram flickered and disappeared.

Rosie thanked the Bone. The pups pondered this new information for a bit.

"Eliana knows how to work well with others. We saw it with our own eyes," said Noodles, finally breaking the silence.

"She was good at it, too," added Clyde.

"Pups," said Rosie, "there's something more there. Maybe she doesn't want to play with teammates because she's scared."

"Scared?" asked Clyde. "Scared of what? There are no boogeymen or fireworks on her team."

"True," said Barkley, "but maybe she's scared of being hurt."

*Hurt.* That was a big word that hit each pup right in their hearts.

"Eliana loves basketball," said Rosie. "She played it all the time with her sister."

"Then her sister left," Noodles reminded them. "So maybe the love and the hurt are all mixed together when Eliana plays."

"And," added Barkley, "maybe she's scared to be teammates with others because in her mind, teammates leave. Like her sister did."

"Pups," said Rosie, "this mission *is* much more than just helping Eliana make the team. I think it is also about helping her forgive her sister and remember how to play as a teammate."

"But how can we do all that with only one more day of tryouts?" asked Clyde.

"Well, we know that sportsmanship means cheering for your teammates and telling them nice things like 'good job!'" began Rosie.

"Yep, tried that," said Barkley. "Paisley got the picture—not Eliana."

"What else can we try?" asked Rosie.

"We know she needs help with passing the ball instead of just shooting it every time," said Clyde.

"That's right!" said Barkley. "Maybe that can be our next plan. Get her to pass the ball. I think I have just the idea of how to do it!"

Day 5 of tryouts couldn't come fast enough! The pups waited behind the bushes. Their plan was ready to go. All they needed was for Eliana to take the court.

The perfect time came right after the first set of drills.

"Okay, girls, time to play ball," called Coach Hampton. "Eliana, you're in!"

"It's showtime!" barked Barkley as he tossed a giant piece of gum into his mouth and began to chew.

"Ready when you are," said Noodles.

After chewing the gum and getting it good

and sticky, Barkley transformed into a ladybug, carrying the wad of sticky gum on his head. He opened his wings and took flight. Noodles blew a wind burst and sent Ladybug-Barkley flying toward the corner of the basketball court. Once there, Barkley dropped the giant wad of gum onto the court. Then he ladybug-scurried back to the bushes as fast as his little buggy legs could go.

"Way to go, Pup!" said Rosie. "Now we watch . . . and wait."

*Tweet* went the coach's whistle and the practice game began. Eliana got the ball and dribbled. This time, Paisley hurried up to her and guarded her. When Eliana went right, Paisley went right. When Eliana went left, Paisley went left. Paisley reached her hands up high, making it hard for Eliana to shoot—but she still didn't pass the ball.

"NOW!" called Rosie.

Noodles kicked up a wind and pushed Eliana to the corner as she dribbled.

And right on cue, Eliana stepped right onto the giant wad of gum. Her foot was stuck and she couldn't move! Plus, Paisley's hands up high made it impossible to take a shot.

Then Annie came up from the side. Eliana positioned herself as if she was about to shoot.

But when she let the ball go, Noodles's perfectly placed wind gust guided the ball, causing it to sail right into Annie's hands. She caught the ball, shot it, and . . . *SWISH!*

But also—*OOF!* With Eliana's foot seemingly glued to the ground, she had fallen right over.

"Ow, ow, ow!" she called, holding her knee. "Owww!"

Each pup sucked in their breath and held it. The gum was supposed to get her to pass, not make her hurt herself.

The coaches and all her teammates raced over as she held her knee in pain.

"You all right?" Coach Wong called. He inspected her knee closely.

Then Lesley and Luna extended their hands and helped Eliana to her feet. They let her lean on them as they got her unstuck and walked with her to the sideline. The two girls even helped her sit down so the coach could inspect her knee once more.

"Let's get some ice on that," he said.

Each teammate patted her back and high-fived her, telling her how great a pass that was.

And even though Eliana's knee was hurting, a small smile slid across her face.

"Thanks," she said.

"She may not have passed it on purpose," said Barkley, watching Eliana interact with the others on the sidelines, "but she sure seems to like the attention from her teammates."

Deidra handed Eliana her water bottle while another teammate brought her a bag of ice for her knee. Then the practice game resumed with someone else taking Eliana's place.

With a curious look glued to her face, Eliana watched the game closely: the shots and passes, the encouragement and high fives, the way the girls all worked together.

"What do you think she's thinking?" Rosie asked.

"I don't know," said Barkley. "But something seems different."

Maybe that something special she'd been missing had finally clicked.

# Chapter 10
# Hard-to-Break Habits

After some time on the sideline, Eliana took the bag of ice and set it aside.

"I'm ready, Coach!" she called.

The pups' tails wagged with anticipation.

When the whistle blew, the ball went sailing

toward Eliana. She grabbed it and shot the ball. *Swish!* Her teammates high-fived her and called out compliments. Eliana glowed, smiling like hearing from these other girls was the best thing ever.

When she got the ball the next time, she shot again—*swish*.

And again—shooting over defenders even though her teammates were open.

"I can't believe it," whispered Rosie. It was still the same old Eliana.

After the fifth shot, fewer teammates high-fived her. And finally, Coach Hampton yelled out: "Remember, girls, you are *nothing* without your team!"

When Eliana got the ball this time, none of her teammates called for it. Nobody looked her way or got in a stance to catch the ball. They just readied themselves to receive a rebound, like they knew she was just going to take the shot again.

"Luna!" called Eliana. The ball went sailing toward her teammate. Luna caught it and shot the basket—*SWISH*. And everybody high-fived her. Even Eliana.

"Great shot," said Eliana.

"Great pass," said Luna, high-fiving her right back.

After the game, Coach Wong called all the girls in.

"That was an excellent game, girls!" he said, bumping fists with each of the girls. "That's what I'm talking about!"

Eliana beamed as her teammates patted her on the back and said nice things.

"Well, Coach Hampton and I both just want to remind you that we'll be posting our final roster tomorrow. Don't feel discouraged if you don't make the team this year. Keep practicing and try out again next year," he said, winking at Eliana.

"Did you see that?" asked Barkley. "Why did he wink at her?"

"Remember," continued Coach Wong, "no practice tomorrow for those of you who made the team. Give yourselves a break, and we'll see the new Lady Gators team on Monday. Really, we've enjoyed working with all of you. Great job out there."

With that, the girls put their hands in and did a final break.

"Why did he wink at Eliana?" Barkley asked again. "Was he saying *she* shouldn't be discouraged? Like maybe, she didn't make the team?"

Was she one of the girls that should try out again next year because she was being cut? Barkley felt the itch come back, like tiny ticks dancing all across his skin.

"Don't think about that now," said Rosie. "All we can do is wait."

* * *

The next day, the pups watched as the coaches taped up their final roster and the girls gathered around the list. Paisley approached, followed by Eliana, who held a basketball under her arm.

Both girls looked down the list for their names.

"Congratulations!" said Paisley. "You're the only third grader on the team!"

"Thanks," said Eliana with a smile. "Congrats to you, too."

"Glad to be your teammate—you've got skills," responded Paisley.

Eliana blushed. "Want to shoot a round?" she asked. "I want to make sure I'm ready for practice on Monday."

"Yeah," said Paisley. "Let's do it, teammate!"

"Okay"—Eliana paused—"teammate!"

The two girls walked over to the court and dropped their bags.

"We did it! We did it!" called Clyde.

"Mission accomplished!" said Rosie. The pups jumped and laughed, landing in a puppy pile with Barkley on the bottom.

Barkley's whole body began to itch even worse. "Got to scratch," he called, using all four paws to relieve the itch. "Got to scratch!"

Each of the puppies jumped off and joined in the scratching party. As they did, Barkley's whole body began to glow from the tip of his nose to the end of his tail.

Then his whole body disappeared.

"Barkley!" called Rosie. "Where did you go?!" Even though she couldn't see him, she could still feel his fur beneath her paws. All the puppies could.

"What do you mean?" asked Barkley. "I'm right here."

In the flick of a tail, Barkley was visible again in his purple body.

"How did you do that?" said Noodles, her

eyes as wide as two big bowls of kibble.

"Do what?" said Barkley, flicking his tail again and disappearing. This time, the pups could see the outline of his body, but it camouflaged perfectly with the grass and bushes around him.

"Barkley Boy," said Rosie, "I think you've gained your new talent!"

"You can disappear!" said Clyde.

"*And* camouflage," added Noodles.

"I can!" he called, flicking his tail once again. "Wow! Amazing!"

"Amazing is right," said Rosie. "You were so worried about getting a new talent. But, Barkley

111

Boy, you've been amazing the whole time. Our team would be nothing without you!"

The pups huddled around Barkley, covering him with puppy kisses. And Barkley smiled his biggest smile yet.

# Chapter 11
# Talents, Teams, and Family

"Three, two, one! Ready or not, here I come!" called Clyde, uncovering his eyes. He flew up into the sky, over the backyard. A glowing light caught his eye. "Found you, Noodles," said Clyde, tagging her as she hid behind a pool chair.

"Did my nose give me away?" she asked. Her excitement caused her nose to glow like a lighthouse.

"Yep! And I see you, too, Rosie," Clyde said, zooming over to a rosebush that he had never seen before.

"You are so good at this game!" said Rosie, laughing loudly.

"But where's Barkley?" All three puppies searched high and low and all around. Even Noodles's nose couldn't pick up Barkley's scent.

"No Barkley here," called Clyde.

Just then, a chuckle came from the hammock.

Barkley's body blinked with light, and he materialized right before their eyes.

"No fair." Clyde laughed. "You blended in with the hammock."

"I guess Hide-and-Seek is out now, too." Barkley laughed.

"We can play a team game," said Rosie. "You know, one where we can cheer one another on."

"You mean, show sportsmanship and teamwork?" said Clyde.

"Exactly," said Barkley.

"This mission really showed me that it takes working together to be successful on a team, even if you already have a lot of talent," said Rosie.

"So true," added Noodles. "And that you should always have a good attitude and tell your teammate nice things like 'good job' or 'you can do it'—even if they make a mistake."

"Yep," added Rosie. "Just like what Coach Hampton said: 'You are *nothing* without your team.' That's the truth! I'm nothing without you pups!"

"Me either," the pups agreed, jumping on one another playfully.

"Also, holding on to hurt feelings can make you stop loving something you really enjoy. But if you let your team in, they'll help you through that hurt," Barkley added. "They'll remind you how amazing you really are."

"Teamwork and sportsmanship can be hard, but they are so important!" added Noodles. "So, what game should we play next?"

"I know," said Clyde. "Why don't we play basketball?"

"Oh, Pups, I almost forgot!" said Rosie. "You just reminded me, Clydie: The Crystal Bone said today is Eliana's first game! We've *got* to see her in action. Come on, let's go!"

The pups bounded through the Doggie Door to Eliana's neighborhood and raced to their regular hiding place next to the blacktop. But it looked different. Lots of people sat around with chairs and hats. Some sat on blankets on the grass. Luckily, the bushes were far enough behind that the pups were still unnoticeable.

Rosie looked around. A row of chairs lined both sides of the blacktop. Eliana and the Lady Gators sat in the chairs on one side, and a different team sat in the chairs on the other side.

Rosie looked at the faces of the people watching.

"They look familiar," said Barkley, pointing to a tall, young-looking woman sitting on a blanket next to an older woman. Both women had brown hair and kind eyes.

Coach Wong called in his players who would start the game, which included both Eliana and Paisley. All the starters high-fived the girls sitting on the chairs, and then one another.

"Let's go, team!" shouted Coach Hampton.

And as the girls lined up for the tip-off, the loud voice of the young woman in the crowd bellowed from the sidelines. "Let's go, Ellie," she sang.

Eliana turned her head and flashed a smile brighter than Noodles's gleaming nose, Rosie's glowing heart, and Barkley's shining body combined. "You got this, Sis!" Marianna called.

*Tweet*! went the whistle, and soon, the ball soared into Eliana's hands.

And Eliana sent it sailing . . . right into the hands of a teammate who waited under the basket. *Swish!*

*Want more Love Puppy magic?*
*Read on for a sneak peek at their next adventure!*

# Chapter 1
# A Dinner Unserved

"Nachos, nachos yeaaaaah," sang Clyde. "I'm gonna eat some nachos, yeah."

Clyde hovered over a small grill where thin slices of steak sizzled and steamed. He took a sniff. The aroma of spices and meat made his

tummy growl and his tail dance. This new recipe was one he had worked on for quite some time, but never got right.

But Clyde was *sure* this time would be just right. Or at least, he hoped.

"Dinnertiiiiiiime," Clyde called to his Love Puppy pals. "I call this *Na-cho Grandpup's Nachos*," he said with a chuckle. "*Bone*-a-petit."

Just as each pup opened their mouths to take giant bites, flashing lights stopped them cold. The Crystal Bone appeared, levitating through the kitchen. A new mission was waiting for them.

"But . . . but—" began Clyde.

"I know, Clydie," said Rosie in a gentle tone. "You worked so hard on this. But dinner will have to wait. Somebody, somewhere, needs our help. Let's go, Pups."

*My Na-cho Grandpup's Nachos would be* nach-so good *if they were cold and soggy,* he thought to himself.

That would be okay, though, if it meant the team would help someone in need. When a mission called, hungry tummies would have to wait.

And with how quickly the Bone alerted the pups, Clyde could tell, this mission was going to be doozie.